MISSING!

Flame

Have you seen this kitten?

Flame is a magic kitten of royal blood, missing from his own world. His uncle, Ebony, is very keen that he is found quickly. Flame may be hard to spot as he often appears in a variety of fluffy kitten colours but you can recognize him by his big emerald eyes and whiskers that crackle with magic!

He is believed to be looking for a young friend to take care of him.

Could it be you?

If you find this very special kitten please let Ebony, ruler of the Lion Throne, know.

Sue Bentley's books for children often include animals or fairies. She lives in Northampton and enjoys reading, going to the cinema, and sitting watching the frogs and newts in her garden pond. If she hadn't been a writer, she would probably have been a skydiver or brain surgeon. The main reason she writes is that she can drink pots and pots of tea while she's typing. She has met and owned many cats and each one has brought a special sort of magic to her life.

Magic Kitten

A Glittering Gallop

SUE BENTLEY

Illustrated by Angela Swan

PUFFIN

PUFFIN BOOKS

UK | USA | Canada | Ireland | Australia
India | New Zealand | South Africa

Puffin Books is part of the Penguin Random House group of companies whose addresses can be found at global.penguinrandomhouse.com.

www.penguin.co.uk
www.puffin.co.uk
www.ladybird.co.uk

First published 2007
This edition published 2016
001

Set in Bembo 15pt/22pt
Printed in Great Britain by Clays Ltd, St Ives plc

A CIP catalogue record for this book is available from the British Library

ISBN: 978–0–141–36783–5

All correspondence to:
Puffin Books
Penguin Random House Children's
80 Strand, London WC2R ORL

www.greenpenguin.co.uk

Conrad – the black-and-white nibbler

⋆Prologue⋆

Lifting his head, the young white lion sniffed the hot breeze rustling through the thorn bushes. It felt good to be home again. Perhaps this time he would be able to stay.

Suddenly a terrifying roar split the air and an enormous black adult lion appeared above him on a rocky ridge.

'Ebony!' Flame gasped, as he looked

up at the terrifying sight of his uncle.

He felt sparks igniting in his fur and there was a bright white flash. Where the majestic young white lion had been, there was now a tiny fluffy calico kitten. Flame edged slowly back into the bushes, hoping that his white fur with ginger and black markings couldn't be seen.

Ebony's fierce eyes looked down, seeming to bore into Flame's tiny kitten body. Flame crouched low, trembling with anger and fear. There was a rustling sound behind him and an old grey lion pushed through the bushes.

'Prince Flame. It is good to see you again. But you have returned at a dangerous time,' Cirrus rumbled.

Flame blinked up at his old friend with relief. 'I am glad to see you too, Cirrus. I had hoped that my uncle would have given up looking for me.'

'That will never happen,' Cirrus told him sadly. 'Ebony is determined to find you and kill you, so that he can keep the throne he stole from you. You must go back to the other world and hide. Use this disguise well and stay safe.'

'I am tired of hiding!' Flame mewed, his emerald eyes flashing. 'I will face my uncle!'

Cirrus showed his worn teeth in a proud smile. 'Bravely said, but first, you must grow strong and wise. Go . . .'

Suddenly another fierce roar rang out. Ebony charged down the rocks and came thundering towards the thorn bushes where Flame and Cirrus were hiding. The ground shook beneath his mighty paws.

'He's seen us! Go now, Flame!' Cirrus urged. 'Save yourself!'

The tiny kitten whined as he felt the power building inside him. His fluffy calico fur glittered with sparks and there was another bright flash. Flame felt himself falling. Falling . . .

⋆Chapter⋆ ONE

Zoe Swann frowned as she looked up at her nan. 'Do I have to?' she grumbled.

Joy Swann smiled, the sunlight glinting on her bright-red hair. 'Don't look so glum, love. Anyone would think I'd asked you to fly to the moon, instead of collect a few eggs!'

Zoe looped the egg basket over her

arm. 'Oh, all right,' she said, pulling a face. 'I suppose I've got to do something, now that Mum's dumped me here!'

Her nan chuckled. 'You know that your mum will write the book more quickly without interruptions. And then she can come down and stay for a few days too.'

'So I'm just an "interruption", am I? Thanks a lot!' Zoe grumbled.

Joy ruffled her granddaughter's short blonde hair. 'Don't be so dramatic, Zoe!'

'Well, it's not my fault if Mum's rotten old book won't behave itself, is it? I promised to creep round the house like a mouse in slippers, but she wouldn't listen,' Zoe said bitterly. Her mum wrote children's books about a family who lived on a barge. They were really good but, to Zoe's annoyance, her mum couldn't have any distractions when writing them – including Zoe.

'It's not for long,' her nan said, her smile wavering. 'You know I love having you to stay and I thought you liked staying with me.'

'I do.' Zoe felt an uncomfortable twinge of guilt. Her nan was great. She was funny and generous and not strict at all. But Zoe had planned to help out at the local stables over the holiday. After each morning mucking out, Lizzie, the stables' owner, let Zoe ride one of the ponies. Now, she was going to miss out on heaps of brilliant rides.

'Off you go then,' her nan said from the back doorstep. 'I'm going inside to do some baking. Oh, by the way. I've just got a new lot of bantams. Watch out for Cocky. He can be a bit bad-tempered.'

'I know how he feels!' Zoe muttered, rolling her blue eyes.

Despite herself, she began swinging her arms as she trudged down her grandmother's endless garden. It was hard to stay grumpy on such a beautiful day. Bees flew back and forth over the colourful flower beds. There was a lovely smell of warm grass cuttings and by the time she reached the sturdy wooden chicken house Zoe had cheered up quite a bit.

She looked curiously at the bantams. They were about half the size of normal chickens. Some of them had bright glossy feathers and delicate legs and others were fat and fluffy and looked like they were wearing baggy feathery trousers.

A handsome black cockerel ran out towards the wire mesh of the outside run that surrounded the chicken house. His bright-red crest was raised and there was a fierce glint in his beady red eyes.

'Hi, Cocky,' Zoe said.

The cockerel snapped his beak and flexed his strong clawed feet.

'OK, I get the message!' Zoe backed away. She went round the chicken house and opened the nest box on the other side. 'Wow! Look at these! I thought eggs were only white or brown!' The bantams' eggs were all shades of pale green, blue and grey. There were even pink ones with little brown freckles.

Zoe filled the basket with eggs and then decided to take the long way back to the house, past the chickens and greenhouse into the orchard.

As Zoe wandered towards the

greenhouse she noticed that the door was open. Inside she glimpsed a jungle-like mass of plants with tomatoes, peppers and lots of stuff she didn't recognize.

Suddenly, from among all the plants, there was a flash of bright white light. 'What was that?' A little nervously, she crept inside.

At first Zoe couldn't see anything odd as she walked between the rows of plants and flowers but just as she was about to turn back, she noticed something glowing faintly at the very back of the greenhouse.

Zoe went forward slowly. As she got closer she saw a big pile of old flowerpots in a corner and on top of them there crouched what appeared to be a tiny kitten. In the light its fluffy coat seemed to sparkle all over. Zoe blinked hard. How did a kitten get in here?

When Zoe looked again, the sparkles seemed to have faded. The kitten was really cute with white fur and ginger and black markings and the brightest emerald eyes Zoe had ever seen.

'What are you doing in Nan's greenhouse?' Zoe said aloud.

The kitten pricked up its tiny ears and looked straight at her. 'I am hiding from my uncle, who wants to kill me,' it mewed.

'Oh!' Zoe dropped the basket of eggs and her hands flew to her face in complete shock.

★Chapter★ TWO

Zoe stared at the calico-coloured kitten in utter amazement. 'Did . . . did you just speak?' she stammered.

The kitten nodded and lifted its tiny chin proudly. 'Yes, I did. My name is Prince Flame, heir to the Lion Throne. What is yours?'

'I'm . . . Zoe. I'm staying here with my nan,' Zoe answered, her mind whirling.

She couldn't believe this was happening, but her curiosity was beginning to get the better of her shock. Bending down, she made herself seem much smaller, so she didn't frighten the amazing kitten away. 'You're a prince? And did you say that someone was trying to kill you?'

'Yes. My uncle Ebony. He has stolen my throne and rules in my place. One day I will return and regain my throne,' Flame mewed, his bright emerald eyes glittering with anger.

'But aren't you much too small to rule anyone?' Zoe asked gently.

Flame said nothing, but his calico fur began to sparkle all over. He jumped off the flowerpots and Zoe was blinded by a bright silver flash.

'Oh!' Zoe rubbed her eyes. When she looked again, she saw that the fluffy kitten had gone. In its place stood a magnificent young white lion.

Zoe gulped. Eyeing the huge paws and sharp teeth, she began to back away slowly.

'Do not be afraid. I will not harm you,' the lion rumbled in a deep velvety roar. There was another flash of light and Flame reappeared as a tiny calico kitten.

'Wow! You really are a lion prince!' Zoe said, relieved and amazed at the same time.

'Yes. I am in disguise,' the tiny kitten mewed, trembling from head to toe. 'I must hide from my uncle's spies. Can you help me, Zoe?'

Zoe felt a second of doubt at the thought of Flame's evil uncle. But then she looked at the gorgeous cute kitten. Flame was awesome as his real self, but in his kitten disguise he looked so helpless and frightened that her generous heart melted.

'Of course I will!' Zoe crooned. She bent down and picked Flame up. 'I'll look after you. Don't you worry about your horrible old uncle. I bet he's no match for my nan! Just wait until I tell her all about you!'

Flame squirmed. He reached up a tiny, white, ginger-tipped paw and stroked Zoe's cheek. 'You must tell no one that I am a prince! It must be a secret!'

Zoe frowned. She knew her nan could be trusted.

'You must promise,' Flame insisted. He blinked at her with wide trusting eyes.

Zoe felt a bit guilty that she couldn't tell her nan, but if it would help to keep Flame safe she was prepared to agree. 'OK, I promise.'

Flame rubbed the top of his fluffy head against her chin. 'Thank you, Zoe.'

'That's OK. Let's go into the house. I expect you're hungry,' Zoe said.

Flame purred eagerly.

Zoe picked up the basket of eggs. Amazingly none of them had broken. She held Flame close with her free hand as she went out of the greenhouse and headed up the garden.

She could still hardly believe that she

had found a magic kitten. With Flame to look after, it looked as if staying with Nan was going to be exciting after all!

'What an absolutely gorgeous kitten and I love his name!' Zoe's nan said as soon as Zoe had introduced Flame. 'Where did you find him?'

Zoe told her about finding Flame in the greenhouse.

Joy Swann frowned. 'Strange. I wonder how he got into the garden. A tiny kitten like that couldn't have climbed the wall.'

'Maybe he crawled under the back gate,' Zoe suggested hurriedly. 'Can I keep him, Nan? I promise I'll look after him. He can live in my room with me.

If you let me keep him I'll feed the chickens, collect the eggs every day and even be nice to stroppy old Cocky!'

Her nan chuckled and gave Zoe's shoulder an affectionate squeeze. 'I'm glad to see that you've cheered up at last. That long face you've been wearing since you arrived would have turned milk sour! Of course Flame can stay. But I'll let the local pet-care centre know and you'll have to be prepared for his owner to claim him.'

Zoe nodded. 'I will. Thanks a million, Nan.' She didn't expect anyone would claim this particular kitten!

While Nan made a quick phone call, Zoe took a tin of sardines from the cupboard and forked them into a dish. 'There you are, Flame.'

Flame purred as he gobbled the sardines hungrily and then sat and licked his whiskers clean.

A few minutes later, her nan came back into the kitchen. 'Now – about all those chores you've promised to do,' she said with a twinkle in her eye.

'Yes?' Zoe said brightly, determined to show that she meant what she'd said.

'I was about to go and pick some raspberries . . .'

'Flame and I will do it.' Zoe jumped up at once and took a plastic bowl from a shelf. 'Come on, Flame!' she called.

Flame scampered outside after Zoe as she took a shortcut across the lawn to the orchard. The late afternoon sun cast long shadows from the apple trees. There was a summer house in one corner and a patch with fruit bushes nearby. Zoe began picking raspberries from their canes. 'I love it down here. It's almost like a secret garden,' she told Flame.

'It is warm and peaceful. I feel safe here,' Flame purred happily, stretching out full length in the warm grass.

Suddenly Zoe saw a flash of reddish-brown and a slim shape dashed through the trees.

'Wow! A fox,' she breathed.

She froze. But the fox had already seen her. It dashed towards the greenhouse and ducked under some bushes.

Flame sat bolt upright and gave an eager little mew.

'Did you see that fox too? Wasn't it gorgeous?' Zoe said excitedly.

Flame didn't answer at first. He stared fixedly at a big twisted tree that was near the garden wall. 'There are some humans over there!'

'Where . . . ?' Zoe began, frowning.

A boy and a girl shot out from behind the tree and hurtled towards the garden wall. They both wore jeans, T-shirts and trainers and looked about ten years old, the same as Zoe.

'Hey!' Zoe yelled, sprinting after them. What a cheek! Those kids must have been trying to pinch her nan's apples!

The kids reached the wall. They scrambled up the uneven stone, as agile as monkeys. The girl reached the top first. She swung her leg over and disappeared down the other side. When the boy got to the top, he crouched there on his knees and glanced over his shoulder.

Zoe caught a glimpse of a thin, worried face, glasses and floppy dark hair.

Suddenly, the boy wobbled. He gave a

yell. Almost in slow motion, he toppled backwards.

'Oh, no! He's falling!' Zoe gasped in horror.

Time seemed to stand still as Flame appeared by Zoe's feet, sparks igniting in his fluffy calico fur and his whiskers crackling with electricity.

A warm tingle flowed down Zoe's spine and she shivered, strangely certain that something was about to happen.

⋆Chapter⋆ THREE

Flame lifted a tiny, white, ginger-tipped paw and a bright stream of sparks shot out from it, hitting an empty sweets bag at the base of the wall.

The bag instantly turned into an enormous pile of giant, squishy, pink marshmallows.

It was only just in time.

'Oof!' The boy landed on the massive marshmallow pile. His glasses pinged off his nose and bounced on to the grass as he sank deeper into the pillowy marshmallows.

Zoe dashed over to him. 'Are you OK?' she asked anxiously.

'I thought I was going to break a leg!' the boy said, sitting up and looking dazed.

'It would have served you right!' Zoe said indignantly to this apple-pinching boy, now that she could see he wasn't hurt.

The boy blinked up at her short-sightedly. 'Who are you? What have I landed on?'

Every time he moved he slid and bounced about on the marshmallows. Pink blobs were stuck all over his hair and face. He looked so funny that Zoe had to bite back a smile.

'Er . . . leaves and grass and stuff!' she improvised, making frantic waving signs to Flame behind her back.

Flame waved his paw again. To Zoe's relief, the pile of marshmallows magically transformed into a big pile of apple-tree leaves. She saw that every bit of pink marshmallow had disappeared from the boy and the sparkles had faded from Flame's fur.

The boy pushed himself on to his knees and started feeling all around. 'Where are my glasses? I can't see a thing without them.'

'Well done, Flame,' Zoe whispered, as she started looking for the glasses.

Flame purred and rubbed himself against her ankles.

Zoe spotted the glasses in a patch of long grass. Picking them up, she handed them to the boy. 'Here you are.'

'Thanks.' The boy put his glasses on and pushed his floppy dark hair out of his eyes. 'Hi! I'm Tod Trapman,' he said, flashing Zoe a grin. 'I live next door. What are you doing here? I haven't seen you before.'

'I'm Zoe. I'm staying with my nan. And this is her garden and you're trespassing!' Zoe said. 'I should report you for stealing her apples!'

'Me and Tod weren't stealing!' called a girl's voice.

Zoe looked up to see a girl perched on top of the wall. She had floppy dark hair too, but hers was long and tied into a ponytail. Except for the glasses, she looked exactly like Tod.

'That's my sister Tracy,' said Tod.

'You're twins,' Zoe said.

'Ten out of ten for observation!' Tracy joked.

Zoe couldn't help grinning. 'Well, anyway, what were you doing in here?'

The twins exchanged wary glances. 'Don't tell her, Tod. I don't think . . .' Tracy began.

'It's OK, Tracy. She helped me just now. I reckon we can trust her,' Tod said.

'We've been coming over here to feed Bracken. We think she's probably had cubs,' he explained.

'Bracken?' Zoe asked, confused.

'The fox that lives near here,' Tracy explained.

Zoe's face lit up. 'Oh! I just saw her!'

Tod nodded. 'She knows us now, but she's still shy of strangers. That's why she ran off when she saw you.'

'She hasn't brought her cubs here yet, but we're sure she will when she thinks it's safe. We're dying to see them,' Tracy added.

Zoe felt excited. It would be great to see Bracken with her cubs.

'That's a really cute kitten. Is it yours?' Tod said suddenly, bending down to stroke Flame's tiny ears. He purred in appreciation.

Zoe nodded. 'Yes. He's called Flame. I, er . . . haven't had him long.' She looked up at Tracy. 'Why do you and Tod come over the wall? It's dead dangerous. I bet my nan would let you use the gate if you asked her.'

'As if!' Tracy scoffed. 'People who have chickens have a real downer on foxes, don't they? She's more likely to want to poison Bracken.'

'She wouldn't!' Zoe cried, horrified. 'Nan loves wildlife. She won't even use slug pellets, in case a hedgehog eats one.'

'Really?' Tod said. 'Maybe we could ask her, Tracy.'

Tracy's eyes blazed. 'No way! You swore we'd keep it a secret! Bracken relies on us and I'm not letting her down. We can't risk it.'

'Hang on, Tracy. I nearly broke my leg falling off the wall today. It would be a lot easier to come in through the garden gate,' Tod said reasonably. 'What about if Zoe puts in a word for us with her nan? Would you, Zoe?'

Zoe thought about it. She decided it would actually be nice to have some people her own age around. 'OK. We can go and ask her now if you like.'

'Ask me what?' said a voice behind Zoe.

Joy Swann came through the trees. 'I came to see why you were taking so long to pick those raspberries.' She looked at Zoe and Tod, who was still stroking Flame. 'Who's your young friend, Zoe?' she asked and then she glanced up at Tracy. 'And would someone like to tell me why there's a girl sitting on the top of my garden wall?'

⋆Chapter⋆ FOUR

'. . . and that's why Tod and Tracy have been climbing into the orchard for the past few weeks,' Zoe finished explaining about Bracken.

Her nan nodded, taking it all in, and then she smiled. 'Well, I must say it's nice to meet my new neighbours at last – even if it is in a rather unusual way! I was wondering who'd moved into the old barn buildings across the back field.'

Tod smiled with relief, but Tracy still looked a little worried. 'You . . . you won't tell our parents about this, will you?' she asked. 'Dad will do his nut if he finds out!'

'As you're not going to be climbing over my wall from now on, I don't think I need to speak to your parents,' Zoe's nan said. 'Now why don't we all go into the house and you can have something to eat while you tell me a bit more about Bracken.'

In the kitchen, Zoe and the twins sat at the kitchen table. Zoe stroked Flame, who was curled up on her lap.

Her nan fetched cool drinks and then passed around a plate piled with warm scones, topped with raspberries and thick fresh cream.

'Wow! Thanks, Mrs Swann,' Tod said, tucking in.

'Call me Joy,' she replied, smiling and listening with interest as the twins told her their suspicions that Bracken had had cubs.

'We've seen her near the allotments at the back of Bants Lane a couple of times. We think she has a den over there,' Tracy told her.

Joy Swann nodded. 'That's a likely place for a fox's den. Some of those allotments are really overgrown. Let me know if Bracken brings her cubs into my garden. I'd love to see them.'

'We will!' chorused Tod and Tracy.

'The old summer house is a good

spot for a night watch, if you fancy one sometime!' Zoe's nan said with a twinkle in her eye.

'Cool!' Tod said.

Tracy's eyes widened in surprise. 'How come you don't mind having a fox coming into your garden? What about your chickens?'

Joy Swann tucked a strand of unruly bright-red hair off her face. 'I built the henhouse myself. The run's fox-proof and I always shut the bantams away at night for good measure. Unless Bracken brings a pair of wire-cutters with her, my chickens are pretty safe!'

Everyone laughed.

'Thanks very much for the scones, Mrs Swann – I mean, Joy,' Tod corrected himself. 'We have to go now.

Our ponies need exercising.'

Zoe was giving Flame a blob of cream on her finger. Her head came up. 'Ponies?'

Tracy nodded. 'We've got three: Fudge, Patch and Ginger. They're gorgeous. Why don't you come over tomorrow and meet them?'

'I'd love to. I'll bring Flame too. Can I, Nan?' Zoe asked eagerly.

'Course you can, love,' her nan said. 'I've got some shopping to do anyway and I don't suppose you're interested in coming with me.'

Zoe grinned. 'Ponies or shopping? Sorry, Nan. It's no contest!'

The following morning Zoe woke up with a strange noise in her ear. It took her a few moments before she realized that it was Flame purring beside her on the pillow.

'Hello, you,' she crooned, tickling him gently under his chin. 'Did you sleep well?'

'Very well, thank you,' Flame purred more loudly.

'We'd better get up. We're going over to Tod and Tracy's, remember?' Zoe threw back the duvet and quickly got dressed.

Downstairs, she fed Flame first and then ate breakfast with her nan. She was in such a good mood that she stacked the breakfast things in the dishwasher without being asked.

Her nan looked pleasantly surprised. 'Thanks, love. Are you ready? I'll walk along the lane with you to Tod and Tracy's. It's on the way to the shops and I thought I'd take them a few raspberries.'

Zoe and Flame followed her outside the front door and they turned immediately left into Bants Lane. Flame scampered along beside Zoe. He nosed about in the long grass, eagerly sniffing all the country smells.

'He's very confident for such a tiny kitten,' Zoe's nan commented.

'Yes, he is.' Zoe smiled, wishing that she could tell her that Flame was really a young white lion!

After a couple of minutes they came to a large fenced field, which followed the curve in the lane. As the lane straightened out, Zoe saw the old barn and the long pebbled drive leading up to it.

'The Trapmans have made a good job of those tumbledown old buildings,' Zoe's nan said, looking at the sparkling honey-coloured stone walls and new roof.

The front door was opened by a slim woman with dark hair, wearing jeans and a pink blouse. 'Hello, you must be Joy Swann and Zoe. Tracy and Tod told me you gave them tea yesterday. That was very kind of you. Come in,' she said with a warm smile.

'Hello, Mrs Trapman,' Zoe said politely.

As Zoe, Flame and her nan went into the kitchen, Tod appeared at the back door wearing jeans tucked into wellington boots. 'Hiya, Zoe!' he said, beaming. 'Come with me. Tracy's in the stables.'

With Flame at her heels, Zoe followed Tod.

'Have a lovely morning with Tod and Tracy. I'll see you later,' her nan called after her.

'What lovely raspberries. Thank you. Have you got time for a cup of tea?' Mrs Trapman asked.

Tod grinned at Zoe. 'Your nan and my mum seem to be getting on OK.'

Zoe nodded. She saw Tracy coming out of the stables wheeling a barrow full of soiled straw and droppings.

Tracy looked up and smiled. 'Hi! I won't be a minute. I'm just going to dump this lot.'

'Can I help?' Zoe offered.

Tracy looked pleased. 'Thanks. You can put down some fresh straw if you like. Tod will show you where things are.'

Tod led the way into the stables. Zoe picked Flame up and followed him. She couldn't wait to meet the ponies. There were six stalls in the stables. Three were empty, but there was a pony in each of the remaining stalls.

'This is Patch,' Tod told Zoe, stroking the first pony's nose.

Zoe saw that Patch was a handsome light bay with a white blaze. Next Tod showed her Ginger, who was also light bay with four white socks. 'And this is dear old Fudge,' Tod said, pointing to a light-brown pony with a pale mane and tail.

'Hello, girl,' Zoe said softly, patting the palomino pony's shoulder. Fudge put her ears forward and whickered a soft greeting.

Out of the corner of her eye, Zoe saw Flame pounce on a wisp of straw. He growled and started play-fighting. 'Don't go too near the ponies' hooves, in case they kick out,' she warned him.

Flame immediately sat down. Looking up at Zoe with bright emerald eyes, he pricked his ears. Fudge swung her head down towards the tiny kitten and gave a friendly snort.

'I reckon that kitten understands every word you say,' Tracy said, coming back into the stables. 'And look at old Fudge. She's really taken to him!'

Zoe smiled secretly to herself. She helped Tod and Tracy put down fresh straw, fill water buckets, and refill hay nets.

Flame found a sunny corner and curled up in the clean hay for a snooze.

'Shall we tack up and take the ponies out now? Do you want to ride Fudge, Zoe?' Tracy said.

'I'd love to!' Zoe exclaimed. She had been hoping the twins would suggest that she ride the palomino pony! Then she remembered something. 'Oh, I didn't bring any riding kit to my nan's.'

'What size shoes do you take?' asked Tracy. Luckily Zoe and Tracy wore the same size. Tracy loaned her a pair of jodhpur boots, a hat and some gloves.

Tracy ran into the house to tell her mum where they were going. When she returned they all mounted. Zoe rode along behind Tod on Patch and Tracy on Ginger. She patted Fudge's smooth warm neck.

It felt wonderful to be riding again. It was her most favourite thing in the whole world. Suddenly she felt her heart miss a beat. Flame! In all the excitement, she had left him behind at the stables!

⋆Chapter⋆ FIVE

Zoe felt terrible. She had to go back for Flame, right now. She was meant to be keeping him safe!

Just as she was about to turn Fudge round, she spotted a familiar little calico-coloured shape beside the track.

'Flame!'

The tiny kitten was running flat out, his paws skimming the ground and his tiny tail stretched right out behind him.

Zoe stopped Fudge. Ahead of her, Tod and Tracy carried on, unaware that she had fallen back.

Flame's fur sparkled as he launched himself straight up into Zoe's arms.

'I am sorry, Zoe!' he panted, purring loudly. 'I only just woke up and realized that you had gone. You like horses very much, don't you?'

Zoe stroked his soft little ears, still feeling guilty. 'Yes, I do. But that's no excuse for leaving you behind,' she whispered. 'I'm really sorry.'

'I am here now,' Flame mewed, settling into her lap as she squeezed her legs against Fudge, urging her on.

Tod was waiting on Patch for Zoe for catch up. 'Anything wrong?' he asked as Zoe rode up to him.

Zoe shook her head. 'Not now,' she murmured.

Flame was perfectly happy, looking all around with alert eyes as they rode along. He didn't seem to mind that she had forgotten him, but Zoe still couldn't forgive herself.

Tod urged Patch on. 'We're turning

on to a wider track up ahead. It leads to Hackleton Firs.'

No one else was around, so Tod, Tracy and Zoe urged their ponies into a trot. Zoe drew level with Tod and rode beside him, while Tracy entered the large area of fir trees ahead of them.

The sun was warm on Zoe's bare arms. It was quiet except for the sound of the ponies' hooves. Tall fir trees stretched overhead and the bridle paths wove through thick bracken.

Zoe saw an older boy on a dark-bay thoroughbred pony coming towards them through the trees. The boy noticed Tracy on Ginger, but instead of slowing down as she would have expected, he urged his pony into a canter.

'What's that rider doing?' Zoe said, puzzled.

'Hey!' Tracy shouted, as the boy on the bigger pony rode so close to her that Ginger laid his ears back and shied to one side.

The older boy ignored her. 'You kids! Get out of my way!' he shouted at Tod and Zoe, as his pony thundered towards them.

Tod and Zoe had stopped their ponies. Tod just managed to pull Patch to one side of the track. Zoe tried to move aside too, but Fudge snorted and pulled at her bit in alarm.

The older boy pulled on the reins and only just managed to avoid jostling Fudge. 'Why didn't you move, you stupid kid?' he shouted.

As Zoe looked up into his mean eyes and set face, her temper rose. 'You could have slowed down. You had plenty of time!' she shouted back.

'You cheeky . . .' The boy's face darkened. He flapped his arms at Fudge. 'Go on! Ya-ah!'

Fudge rolled her eyes in fright. She leapt forward, crashing through the tall ferns that lined the track.

Flame yowled fearfully. He dug in his claws and hung on to the saddle.

Zoe pulled at the reins, but Fudge was terrified by the bracken stems lashing against her legs and belly. Suddenly a low thorny hedge appeared in front of her. Zoe's heart rose into her mouth. Fudge didn't slow down. She was going to crash into it!

*

Sparks ignited in Flame's calico fur and his whiskers crackled with electricity. A tingling sensation prickled down Zoe's back.

Flame raised a tiny paw and a snowstorm of glitter whirled round Zoe and Fudge.

Three strides, two strides, one stride . . .

Zoe flinched and then gasped as Fudge soared high into the air on a curving bridge of silvery glitter. The pony cleared the hedge easily and landed safely on the bridleway on the other side. Fudge came to a stumbling halt and stood there trembling.

'Thanks, Flame! You were brilliant!' Zoe said shakily, giving him a hug before stroking Fudge's neck to calm the old pony down.

'You are welcome,' Flame purred. Sparks still twinkled in his fluffy fur as he leapt down on to the track like a tiny comet.

Zoe smiled at him, even more determined now to look after this amazing, magic kitten and keep him safe.

'Zoe! Are you all right?' shouted Tracy, interrupting her thoughts as she rode towards her. Tod was just behind his twin.

Zoe quickly glanced at Flame, but the sparks had all faded from his fur.

'We saw Fudge bolt and cut across to head you off!' Tod called.

'I'm fine and Fudge's OK too,' Zoe

said. 'She . . . er, jumped the hedge.' Tod and Tracy looked at each other in amazement. 'Old Fudge jumped that hedge?'

Zoe nodded. *With a bit of help from Flame!* she thought gratefully. 'That horrible boy deliberately startled her. It's lucky Fudge wasn't badly hurt.'

'That was Jake Fawsley. He's a real pain,' Tracy said.

'Does he live around here?' Zoe asked.

Tod nodded. 'His dad's Master of the Hounds for the local drag hunt. He's a really nice man, but Jake's full of himself and thinks he can do just what he likes!'

Zoe remembered the glimpse of the older boy's mean face. 'Shall we carry on with our ride? I don't see why that rotten bully should spoil it for us!'

'Definitely!' Zoe and Tod agreed.

Zoe bent down and lifted Flame carefully up on to Fudge's back and then remounted. Flame purred contentedly in Zoe's lap as she and the twins rode along the bridleways and eventually emerged back out on to the fields.

⋆Chapter⋆ SIX

When they got back Tod, Tracy and Zoe untacked the ponies and turned them out into their paddock and then Zoe and Flame went back to her nan's for lunch.

'Did you have a good time with the twins?' Joy Swann asked her granddaughter.

'Yes, we went riding in the Firs.

I think Flame really enjoyed it too,' Zoe said.

She didn't mention Jake Fawsley or Fudge bolting, as she had a sneaking feeling that she might not be allowed to go riding again.

'Can I open a tin of tuna for Flame, Nan?' Zoe asked. *He deserves a special treat after the way he saved Fudge and me*, she thought.

After lunch, Zoe did a few boring chores for her nan, and then spent a few hours in the garden with Flame. She dragged a twig around for him to chase for a while and then he stretched out beside her while she read a magazine.

It was just starting to get dark when the twins arrived with some food for

Bracken. Zoe and Flame went down to the orchard with them and helped scatter the food within sight of the old summer house. Zoe felt a flicker of excitement as she prepared for her first evening fox-watching with the twins.

They all made themselves comfortable and then sat looking out into the gathering dusk.

'How do you like fox-watching so far?' Zoe whispered after a few minutes to Flame as he curled up beside her on the warm floorboards.

'I like it very much,' he mewed softly.

Tod and Tracy sprawled on their stomachs side by side, peering at the orchard through the open doorway. 'I wonder if Bracken will bring her cubs tonight,' Tod said.

'Oh, I hope so,' Zoe said eagerly.

After about half an hour, when Bracken still hadn't arrived, Tod sat up and pushed back his floppy dark fringe. 'Tracy and I had a brilliant idea earlier,' he told Zoe. 'We've got something to ask you.'

'Have you?' Zoe said, intrigued.

'Yes. We're riding in a gymkhana at the town show next weekend. We wondered if you'd like to go in for it with us,' Tod said.

'You could ride Fudge,' Tracy added. 'That jump yesterday was dead impressive! I don't know how you got her to do it. She's such a sweet lazy old thing.'

'I'm not sure I could do it again,' Zoe said, biting back a smile. She wished she could tell them how Flame had saved them by getting Fudge over the hedge himself, but a promise was a promise. 'I'd love to ride in the gymkhana!'

'Great!' chorused the twins.

Zoe laughed.

'If you come over tomorrow,' said Tod, 'you can help us put up a course of jumps in the field. We can practise together every day until the show.'

Zoe grinned. 'Brilliant! Did you hear that, Flame?'

Flame gave an eager little mew.

Tracy chuckled. 'He just answered you!'

'Shhh! I just saw something over by the greenhouse,' Tod whispered.

Zoe watched closely as a slim red shape emerged from a bush near the greenhouse and began weaving towards them through the shadowy trees. 'It's Bracken!'

Her eyes widened. She had never been so close to a real live fox. Bracken was smaller than she remembered, with a delicate muzzle and a black tip to her tail. She had slender limbs and moved more like a cat than a dog.

Bracken went straight to the food spread on to the grass and began eating hungrily.

'Still no sign of any cubs,' Tracy whispered disappointedly.

'At least we can keep a proper watch,' Tod whispered back. 'When she does bring them, we'll be waiting.'

By the time Bracken had finished eating, the moon had risen, silvering the grass and casting the trees into pools of deeper shadow. The fox slipped away as silently as she had arrived.

Tracy and Tod stood up and stretched. Zoe and Flame walked down to the garden gate with them.

'See you tomorrow,' the twins called as they went out into the lane.

'You bet,' Zoe said, waving. She was really looking forward to putting up the jumps and riding Fudge again. 'Come on, Flame. Let's go in and tell Nan that we've seen Bracken.'

Bright and early the next day, Zoe and Flame walked up Bants Lane to the Old Barn. Tod and Tracy were already in the field, putting out jumps.

Zoe helped with the jumps. She couldn't believe how well her holiday was turning out – not only was she able to do some riding after all, but she had Flame with her too: her own magic kitten!

At last, after mucking out and grooming, the ponies were saddled up. Flame climbed up a fence post and settled down to watch.

Tod and Tracy were experienced jumpers. Their ponies, Patch and Ginger, even seemed to enjoy going over the low jumps. Zoe felt her stomach clench with nerves when it was her turn. She hadn't done much jumping and Flame couldn't use his magic to help her with the twins watching.

She pointed Fudge towards the first jump. What if Fudge was nervous after her fright in the Firs yesterday? Fudge eyed the jump. She started to slow down.

Zoe clicked her tongue. 'Come on, girl!' she said firmly, pressing her on.

Fudge tossed her head. She sped up again and suddenly they flew over the jump.

'Hurrah!' yelled the twins. 'Well done, Zoe!'

Zoe beamed at them. After that, Fudge seemed to get her confidence. She went over all the jumps perfectly. As she trotted back past the fence where Flame was crouched watching, Fudge twitched her ears and gave a friendly whicker.

Flame sat upright and miaowed loudly.

'Look at that. They're saying hello to each other!' Tod said, laughing.

Zoe smiled to herself. The kitten and pony had become good friends. She suspected that Fudge somehow knew that Flame had saved her from getting hurt when she had bolted up at the Firs.

Over the next few days, Zoe and

Flame spent most of the day at the Trapmans' house. With all the practice, Zoe gained confidence and Fudge was now responding to her really well. She couldn't wait to take part in the gymkhana.

One evening, Tod, Tracy, Zoe and Flame were all on fox-watch in Nan's summer house as usual. They had seen Bracken incredibly close almost every evening, but still hadn't seen any sign of her cubs.

Zoe watched Bracken appear from behind the bush near the greenhouse. She noticed that the vixen seemed very wary. Instead of eating the food straightaway, she sniffed it and then lifted her head and looked all around.

'She's acting a bit odd,' Zoe whispered.

'Zoe's right. Why isn't Bracken eating the food?' Tracy said.

Bracken lifted her delicate muzzle and sniffed the air. She gave a low cry.

Tod frowned and pushed his glasses on to the bridge of his nose. 'That's strange. She seems to be calling to someone. You know what I think . . .'

'Yes!' Tracy and Zoe leaned forward eagerly, with shining eyes.

Two small red shapes came out of the bush. The cubs were about half the size of their mother, with thick bushy tails. They crept forward hesitantly and trotted through the orchard. When they reached the food they began eating, watched over by Bracken.

'Oh, aren't they gorgeous!' Zoe whispered in awe.

She and Flame, and the twins, watched as the cubs finished eating and then played a game of tag. Bracken stood by as they rolled around play-growling. Even when she led the way out of the garden the cubs gambolled along after her, trying to bite her tail.

Tod, Tracy and Zoe fell about laughing. 'The little rascals!'

Later, after telling her nan all about the wonderful cubs, Zoe went up to her room. She opened the window and leaned out on to the moonlit garden.

'Clever Bracken! Two healthy cubs,' she said, yawning. 'I wonder if her den is on the allotments. Maybe we could all ride over and have a look sometime. What do you think, Flame?' she asked sleepily.

There was no answer.

Zoe turned back into the room to where Flame's tiny form was curled up on her bed. His whiskers twitched and his tiny paws flexed as he slept. Was he dreaming of his own world and the Lion Throne, which he would one day claim?

She felt a surge of affection for him. She hoped it would be a very long time before he had to leave.

⋆Chapter⋆ SEVEN

Zoe narrowly avoided the cockerel's sharp beak as she tipped out the last of the corn. Stepping outside the chicken run, she shut the door tightly.

'That Cocky's a nightmare,' she said to Flame. 'It's a good thing that you stayed outside the run.'

Flame gave Cocky a wary glance before following Zoe to the feed shed.

The cockerel was almost twice his size.

'Right. Chores finished. I'll just go and tell Nan that we're going over to see the twins.' A gust of cool wind ruffled Zoe's short hair as she closed the door of the shed and she zipped up her bodywarmer.

'I like to ride with you, Zoe,' Flame purred.

Zoe picked him up and gave him a cuddle. 'You like old Fudge, don't you? She's fond of you too.'

When Zoe and Flame got to the Old Barn, Tod and Tracy already had the ponies saddled up. 'We thought we'd go out for a ride instead of practising jumping this morning,' Tracy said.

'Fine by me,' Zoe said, lifting Flame up on to Fudge, before mounting. 'Can we go past the allotments? I was thinking we might see Bracken.'

'Good idea,' Tod said.

They rode down the drive and carefully crossed Bants Lane. After passing a row of houses, they turned on to a track that led along the side of the allotments.

Flame was snuggled inside Zoe's bodywarmer, with just his head poking out. As she rode, Zoe glanced towards a tangled hedge of hawthorn. There was a flash of red as a fox darted into the bottom of the hedge.

Zoe stiffened. 'Look! Over there!'

Tod and Tracy had seen Bracken too.

'You were right about her den. It must be somewhere near that hedgerow,' Tod said. 'We'd better not go any nearer or it might scare the cubs.'

They continued riding along the track, which opened out on to some fields. After about an hour, they turned back and retraced their steps.

As they came back towards the allotments, Zoe was riding alongside Tracy. She heard the baying of hounds.

'That's Mr Fawsley exercising the pack. I bet Jake's with him,' Tracy said. She didn't look very pleased at the idea of seeing the unpleasant lad again.

Zoe didn't fancy meeting him again either. She still felt angry at the way Jake had deliberately startled Fudge.

The baying was getting louder. Zoe felt a flicker of alarm. The hounds were coming this way! 'What about Bracken and her cubs!' she cried.

'If they get the scent of a fox, he'll never be able to call them off,' Tod said.

'We have to ask Mr Fawsley to take the hounds somewhere else!' Zoe said urgently, pressing Fudge into a trot.

Plunging forward, she sped down the track. As she rounded a bend, she came upon the pack of milling hounds cutting across a field towards her. She pulled on Fudge's reins and the pony slowed to a halt.

'There's a fox and her cubs on the allotments. Can you turn the hounds round, please, Mr Fawsley!' she called breathlessly to a tall dark man in a tweed jacket.

Mr Fawsley was surrounded by the pack of big handsome hounds, all wearing wide doggy grins and wagging their tails. There was a lad with him. Zoe recognized him. It was Jake.

Mr Fawsley looked up at Zoe and gave a friendly smile. 'Hello, there! What's that about a fox?'

'Leave it to me, Dad. I met this cheeky kid the other day,' Jake said curtly, striding up to Zoe.

'Yes, at Hackleton Firs, when you nearly rode me down!' Zoe flashed at him. 'Fudge bolted because of you. We could both have been badly hurt!'

'Is this true, Jake?' his father asked sternly.

Jake swallowed. 'Course not. What do you take me for?'

Zoe gaped at Jake, shocked by the blatant lie, but there wasn't time to argue. 'Please can you turn back the hounds, Mr Fawsley? Bracken, a fox we know, has a den with cubs in it on the allotments.'

'Oh, right. Thanks for . . .'

Before his father could finish speaking, Jake roughly grabbed Fudge's bridle. 'Tough! We've got a right to cut through the allotments if we feel like it!' he sneered at Zoe.

'Jake! There's no need for that!' rapped Mr Fawsley.

Jake ignored his father and tugged at Fudge's bridle. The pony laid her ears back and took a step backwards.

From inside her bodywarmer, Zoe heard an indignant miaow, as sparks lit up in Flame's fur and his whiskers glowed with power. Zoe felt the familiar tingling down her spine. *Now you've done it, Jake Fawsley*, she thought.

Jake's eyes widened in surprise. 'Ye-ow! That's hot!' he yelled, jerking his hand back from Fudge's bridle. Suddenly, he flew backwards as if he had been shot out of a cannon, and sat down hard on his bottom.

'Well done, Flame!' Zoe whispered.

By now Tod and Tracy had caught Zoe up. When they saw Jake sitting on the floor, they both started laughing.

Jake snarled, rubbing his sore hand. His face was as red as a beetroot as he started to get up. 'I'll get you for that . . .'

Mr Fawsley strode forward, grabbed his son by the collar and heaved him to his feet. 'That's enough, Jake! Help me with the hounds!' he ordered. 'And I'll have something to say to you later!' He looked at Zoe. 'I apologize for my lout of a son, young lady. Don't worry. I'll deal with him!'

Tod, Tracy and Zoe sat on their ponies and watched as Mr Fawsley and Jake controlled the pack. In a couple of minutes, the hounds had turned round and gone streaming back across the fields with Mr Fawsley and Jake walking along in the middle of them.

'I reckon Jake's in for a severe telling-off!' Tod said, chuckling.

'Serves him right,' Zoe said heatedly. 'Maybe he'll think twice before trying to bully anyone else!'

Tracy shrugged. 'I wouldn't count on it. Jake's the type to try to get even.'

'Huh! Just let him try. I'm not scared of him!' Zoe said angrily. *Not while I've got Flame on my side!* she thought.

★Chapter★ EIGHT

Zoe's mum phoned a couple of evenings later to say that she had almost finished her book. 'I'll be there by the weekend,' she told Zoe.

'Great! You can watch me in the gymkhana,' Zoe said delightedly.

'Your nan told me that you'd made friends with her new next-door neighbours. It sounds as if you're having a great time with the twins and their ponies. You certainly don't sound like the grumpy girl I know who can sulk for England!' she teased.

'I don't know who you're talking about!' Zoe said, trying not to laugh. 'I'm glad the writing's going well. See you soon, Mum. Bye!'

As soon as she put the phone down, she went to find Flame.

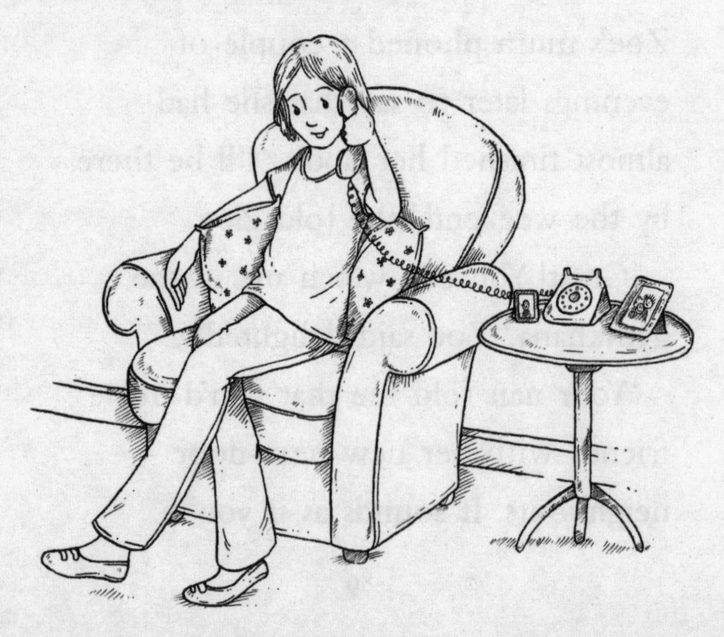

He was curled up on a kitchen chair, snoozing after finishing his supper.

Zoe bent down. 'Wake up, sleepyhead,' she whispered gently, stroking his soft fur and breathing in his sweet kitten smell. 'We're going down to the summer house. I told Tod and Tracy we'd meet them there.'

Flame yawned, showing his sharp little teeth. He mewed eagerly and jumped down to follow Zoe.

Zoe loved it in the garden as dusk fell. In the soft light, everything looked so fresh and bright. She and Flame padded down the path that led past the henhouse and greenhouse and then curved round to the orchard. Flame scampered ahead to bat at a butterfly with one soft paw as it flew up from a buttercup.

Zoe chuckled at Flame's cute antics. Sometimes she almost forgot that he was really a magnificent lion prince.

There was a bantam hen on the path ahead. It was scratching about looking for grubs. There was another one, further down the path.

Zoe stopped in surprise. She was sure Nan had shut all the bantams in the henhouse for the night. Nan was very careful about that, especially now that Bracken and her cubs were visiting the garden.

Just then Cocky strutted towards her from the direction of the orchard. His red crest stood up and he ruffled his black wing feathers menacingly.

'What's going on?' Zoe said, looking around in puzzlement.

Suddenly she noticed that the door to the chicken run was wide open. Someone must have deliberately let out all Nan's bantams!

Zoe heard a faint scrabbling sound. She spun round and was just in time to see a dark shape disappearing over the garden wall. It looked like Jake Fawsley. She thought of dashing to the gate and running after him, but it was more important to get the bantams to safety.

'We have to get them all back inside the henhouse before Bracken discovers them,' she said to Flame. 'No fox, especially one with cubs, is going to be able to resist an easy meal!'

Zoe dashed forward and made a grab

at one of the bantams. Squawking loudly, it fluttered over a bush. She lunged at another one, but it avoided her easily. Cocky gave her a stern look from his beady red eyes that seemed to say, 'Don't even try it!' Zoe groaned. 'This is hopeless! I'll never catch them all like this!'

'Do not worry, Zoe. I will help,' Flame purred.

Big silver sparks glowed in Flame's calico fur and his whiskers glittered with electricity, lighting up the dark garden. Zoe felt her spine tingle as she wondered excitedly what was about to happen.

Flame pointed a tiny paw at a garden rake, which was leaning against the side of the nearby greenhouse. A big fountain of sparks whooshed out. There was a loud popping sound and the rake turned into a huge, long-handled fishing net.

'Brilliant!' Zoe said, grabbing it in two hands, realizing what Flame meant her to do.

Zoe ran to a tree, where a couple of bantams had fluttered up on to a low branch. Swish! She scooped them straight into the net, before quickly shutting them away and going in search of the others.

By the time she had swiped up the rest of the hens and shut them away safely, Zoe was bright red and out of breath. 'Phew! Everyone's safe – except for Cocky! Now – where is he?'

Flame stood beside her with his ears pricked, looking around helpfully. 'I cannot see him.'

Suddenly there was a screech as Cocky launched himself out of an apple tree, straight at Flame. His strong clawed feet flexed and he snapped his beak menacingly.

Flame cringed, completely taken by surprise by Cocky's attack.

Zoe didn't have the space to swing the net at the angry bantam cock. There was no time to think. Dropping the net, she launched herself at Cocky and grabbed him in both hands. She wasn't going to let anything hurt Flame!

Cocky squealed with rage, thrashing his feet.

'Oh!' Zoe gasped with pain, as the razor-sharp claws and spurs raked her chest. Somehow she managed to keep hold of Cocky and stagger with him to the chicken run. She opened the door with her elbow, threw the cockerel inside, and latched the door.

Zoe's knees gave way and she sank on to the grass in shock. The front of her T-shirt was all ripped. Waves of pain radiated from the deep scratches.

'You saved my life, Zoe. But you are hurt!' Flame mewed in concern.

'It doesn't matter. It was worth it,' Zoe said bravely, biting her lip. Tears filled her eyes and for one horrible moment, she thought she was going to faint.

Flame's calico fur glittered once more with bright sparks. He leaned forward and very gently breathed out a stream of twinkling rainbow mist.

Warmth seemed to flood over Zoe's chest and she gasped. The scratches tingled sharply for a few seconds and then all of a sudden the pain quickly faded. Zoe put her hands up to her chest. The rips in her T-shirt had mended themselves too.

She gathered Flame into her arms. 'Thanks, Flame. I don't know what I'd do if anything happened to you,' she crooned.

Flame gave an extra-loud purr and rubbed his head against her chin. As she stroked him, the last sparks in his fur fizzed against her fingers and went out.

'What are you two doing?' called a cheery voice from behind Zoe.

Tod and Tracy stood there with a bag of leftovers for Bracken and her cubs.

Zoe jumped to her feet with Flame in her arms. 'I'll tell you on the way to the summer house!'

Tracy and Tod listened as Zoe told them about the bantams being let out and the shadowy figure she had seen scrambling over the garden wall.

'It had to be Jake Fawsley. The rotten beast!' Tracy burst out.

'I haven't got any proof that it was him,' Zoe said reasonably.

'Maybe not. But who else could it have been?' Tod asked.

Zoe shrugged. 'I don't know. Anyway, Flame helped me . . . I mean I . . . er, managed to get all the bantams back in, so Jake's plan to get even didn't work.'

'I still think we should phone Mr

Fawsley. And I don't care if it means being a snitch!' Tracy stormed.

'He'd only deny it was him, just like he lied about making Fudge bolt. And it would be his word against ours,' Zoe sighed.

The twins looked at each. They knew Zoe was right.

No one spoke for a while. A few minutes later Bracken and her cubs appeared through the trees and the horrible thought of Jake Fawsley was pushed to the back of everyone's mind.

⋆Chapter⋆ NINE

'I can't believe it's the town show tomorrow!' Zoe said to her nan at lunchtime the following day.

Joy Swann smiled and handed Zoe a plate of ham salad. 'It's exciting, isn't it? Your mum's arriving first thing, so she can watch you in the gymkhana. And I think I've a good chance of getting first prize for my bantams this year.'

After lunch, Zoe and Flame went over to the twins' house. They spent the afternoon practising over the jumps and then left the ponies out in the paddock.

Zoe went into the tack room with Tod and Tracy. They all set to, cleaning and polishing until their arms ached. Everything had to be gleaming for tomorrow's show.

Flame curled up on the old wooden chest, where the horses' brushes and clean saddle cloths were kept. Zoe noticed that he kept looking round anxiously. Once he stood up and stared into space, the hackles on his back rising.

Zoe felt a flicker of alarm. What was wrong with him?

Flame insisted on getting into her shoulder bag for the short walk back down the lane to Nan's house. Tucking himself into a small tight ball, he pressed himself into the corner of Zoe's bag.

She slipped her hand inside to stroke him. He was trembling all over. 'What's wrong, Flame?' she asked worriedly.

'I sense my enemies drawing closer. I may have to leave in a hurry,' Flame whined softly.

'Oh, no,' Zoe said, feeling her heart sink.

She had hoped that this day would never come. Now it looked as if Flame might have to leave at any moment. She didn't know how she was going to cope with losing him.

Zoe felt distraught for the rest of the evening as Flame was clearly terrified. She didn't know what to do, except stroke him reassuringly. That night, Flame crawled trembling into the back of Zoe's wardrobe and stayed there, as Zoe lay awake for a long time worrying about him.

★

The following morning, however, Zoe was awakened by a little furry head nudging her cheek. Flame was on her bed. His emerald eyes glowed and he seemed just like his usual self.

'Oh, Flame! You're still here!' Zoe sat up sleepily and gathered him into her arms. She had been almost certain that he'd be gone when she woke up.

'My enemies have passed close by, but they couldn't find me. I think I am safe again for a little while,' Flame purred, snuggling up to her.

'I'm so glad,' Zoe said with relief. She just hoped his enemies kept on going and never came back.

'Zoe! Are you awake?' a familiar voice called up the stairs.

'Mum!' Zoe leapt out of bed. She

hopped about on one foot as she hurriedly pulled on her jeans and then dragged a brush through her short hair. 'Come on, Flame!' she called, racing downstairs.

She threw herself at her mum and gave her an enormous hug.

Zoe's mum smiled. 'I've missed you too! Oh, this must be the kitten I've heard so much about!' She bent down to stroke Flame. 'Hello, little one.'

Flame gave a little mew of greeting. He rubbed his small furry body against Helen Swann's ankles.

'I've a feeling he might be coming home with us?' Helen said to Zoe.

'Definitely!' Zoe said. She promised herself to keep her fingers and toes crossed that Flame would.

Flame padded after Zoe and her mum as they went into the kitchen where Zoe's nan had breakfast ready. As soon as they had all finished eating, it was time to get ready for the town show.

'Who wants to help me bath the chickens?' Joy Swann asked, tying a bright-yellow headscarf over her hair.

Zoe's mum pulled a face. 'That's not something you get asked every day.'

'Come on, Mum, don't be "chicken"!' Zoe giggled. 'I wish I could help, but I have to go and get the ponies ready with Tod and Tracy.' She had arranged to go to the show with the twins and their parents in their smart horse transporter.

Her mum smiled. 'Off you go then,

love. Your nan and I will see you at the show.'

Flame trotted at Zoe's heels as she went out of the back garden gate and into the lane.

Neither of them noticed the long dark shapes that prowled among the trees in the orchard. 'He is very close. We will soon have him!' growled a cold voice.

'Ebony will reward us well,' snarled another.

Zoe leaned forward excitedly as the Trapmans' horse transporter turned into the showground. Flame was on her lap, peering out curiously from inside her shoulder bag.

'Wow! It's much bigger than I expected!' She craned her neck, looking at all the white marquee tents, arenas and show pens.

'I've got butterflies in my tummy,' Tracy moaned.

'You're lucky. I've got whopping great bats in mine!' Tod said.

Mr Trapman parked in the lorry park and Zoe helped the twins get the ponies down the ramp. Flame sat down near Fudge, watching as Zoe groomed her and tacked up. Eventually all the ponies were ready.

Tod, Tracy and Zoe changed into matching white shirts, jodhpurs, boots and hats.

'We've still got an hour before the gymkhana. What shall we do?' asked Tod.

'We could go and see how my mum and nan are getting on with the bantams,' Zoe suggested.

She held her shoulder bag open, so that Flame could jump in. Shouldering the bag, she walked across the showground with the twins. As they neared the poultry marquee, a tall boy in riding gear came out.

It was Jake Fawsley.

'Well, if it isn't that interfering kid again!' he sneered at Zoe. 'I've just seen your nan get first prize. I was surprised she had any bantams left to show. How many did the fox get?'

'So it *was* you who let them all out the other night!' Zoe cried, bunching her fists. 'What a hateful thing to do! I've a good mind to go and tell your dad what you've been up to!'

Jake sniggered. 'I'd like to see you try to prove it!' He walked off, whistling to himself.

Zoe stared after him, fuming.

Tod and Tracy linked arms with her. 'Jake's not worth it. Dad says people like him get what they deserve in the end,' Tod said.

'That's true,' Tracy agreed. 'Come

on, let's go and congratulate your nan.'

'OK,' Zoe said. She put her hand into her bag. As she stroked Flame's soft fur, she felt herself starting to calm down.

Zoe's nan and mum greeted Zoe and the twins with proud smiles. There was a colourful rosette pinned to Cocky's cage. 'Well done, Nan!' Zoe said giving her a big hug. 'Isn't it great, Mum?'

'Wonderful! I'm so proud of her,' Helen Swann said. 'I'm looking forward to seeing you now. How long is it before the gymkhana?'

'About half an hour,' Zoe told her.

'I'll see you over there then,' her mum said. She pressed some money into Zoe's hand. 'Why don't you go and get yourselves an ice cream?'

'Thanks, Mum!' Zoe called over her shoulder, already making for the ice-cream van.

She, Tod and Tracy bought double cones. They ate them hungrily as they wandered towards the showjumping enclosure. Flame stuck his head out of the bag, looking at all the interesting sights. Zoe gave him some ice cream on the end of her finger and giggled as his rough little tongue tickled her.

Zoe suddenly saw a rider on a familiar dark-bay pony who was just beginning his showjumping round. 'Look! It's Jake! Let's go and watch him.'

They all went and stood by the fence as Jake rode over the jumps. Zoe put her bag on the ground so that Flame could get out and stretch his legs.

Jake's pony cleared the first few jumps easily. But on the next jump, Jake turned his pony sharply as it landed.

'He's misjudged that! There's not room for the pony to get a good run at the jump,' Tod said, as Jake approached the water jump. 'If he's not careful, the pony will stop before it jumps and he'll get a refusal.'

The bay pony ran towards the fence. It laid its ears back and faltered. 'Go on!' Jake shouted, slapping it hard on the rump.

The pony threw down its head and came to a sudden dead halt. Jake shot over its neck and landed head first in the water. He stood up with water and mud dripping down his face.

'Oh, bad luck!' Zoe shouted cheerfully.

The twins were openly laughing. 'It couldn't have happened to a nicer person!' Tracy said loudly.

Jake glared over at them. He opened his mouth as if about to say something, but then seemed to remember all the people watching. His shoulders sagged as he squelched round the jump and picked up his pony's reins. His face was as red as a tomato.

Still chuckling, Zoe bent down to pick up her bag. She wondered if Flame had had anything to do with the hilarious scene!

'Did you . . .' she began to ask him in a whisper.

But Flame wasn't inside. Zoe looked all around, but could see no sign of the tiny calico kitten. Strange. Flame had never gone off without telling her where he was going before, especially as he knew how bad she felt for forgetting him that one time when she had been riding Fudge. A dreadful suspicion built inside her and her heart thudded.

Zoe hurried towards a nearby

marquee, looking round desperately for Flame. As she rounded the tent's side, there was a blinding silver flash. Zoe rubbed her eyes and saw that Flame stood there, looking magnificent as his true lion self. Silver sparkles glittered in his thick white fur. There was an older grey lion standing next to him.

'I'm sorry. They have come back,' Flame's deep voice rumbled sadly.

And then Zoe realized that Flame must leave. However much she adored him, he couldn't stay and be in danger from his enemies.

She ran forward and threw her arms round Flame's muscular neck. 'Take care! I'll never forget you!' she said tearfully. She forced herself to stand back. 'Go! Quickly! Save yourself!'

Flame nodded. 'You have been a good friend. Be well, Zoe.'

The old grey lion bowed his head and there was another bright flash and a shower of sparks that crackled in the grass around Zoe's feet. Flame and the grey lion faded and then disappeared.

Zoe stood there, her heart aching and her throat tight with tears.

'There you are!' called Tracy, running up to her. 'Come on. The gymkhana's about to start!'

Zoe rubbed her eyes. She knew that she would never forget the adventure she had shared with the magic kitten. She could never tell anyone about him, but he would be her special secret, forever.

She whirled round to Tracy, feeling excitement starting to push away the sadness. 'Wait for me!' she called.

Wordsearch Wonder

This wordsearch is about Flame's adventures in **A Glittering Gallop.** Remember words may be hidden forwards, backwards, up, down or diagonally.

PONIES	**TROT**
GALLOP	**REINS**
STABLE	**JODPHURS**
SHOWJUMPS	**GYMKHANA**
SADDLE	**PALOMINO**

O	S	A	C	I	D	S	E	I	N	O	P
E	R	C	I	L	I	S	D	U	I	S	A
G	S	N	I	E	R	E	L	D	D	A	S
Y	A	T	I	E	E	U	F	A	C	V	P
M	C	C	A	M	A	P	I	T	U	L	M
K	R	S	I	B	O	T	D	I	G	N	U
H	R	T	I	L	L	A	C	S	U	M	J
A	O	L	L	T	P	E	L	E	D	A	W
N	D	A	R	M	C	O	R	E	D	I	O
A	G	O	S	S	I	B	O	R	E	E	H
M	T	Y	R	J	O	D	P	H	U	R	S
G	U	I	S	O	N	I	M	O	L	A	P

Answers on last page

Mixed-up Magic Words

The answers to all these questions can be made using only the letters in the words:

MAGIC KITTEN FLAME

Where we go to watch movies and eat popcorn.

2 You can make someone giggle by giving them a . . .

The opposite of male.

Something that attracts metal.

5 A warm and woolly item of clothing worn on your hand. ☐☐☐☐☐☐

6 The average weather conditions in a place. ☐☐☐☐☐☐☐

7 A heavenly being with a halo. ☐☐☐☐☐

8 Something that isn't genuine or is a copy. ☐☐☐☐

Answers on last page

Flame meets many other animals on his adventures. A new encounter can be quite a surprise!

★★ 1 ★★

When he first saw a chicken:
'Oo-er – what are those fluffy things with wobbly bits on their heads and sharp pointy things on their noses? We don't have those in my home world! Help – one of them is chasing me!'

When he first saw a fox:
'Is it a cat or a dog? It walks like a cat, but it has a longer face and a really bushy tail. And I'm sorry to have to say this, but I cannot lie. It's a teeny bit ... smelly.'

The second time he saw the same fox:
'Oh, a female, called Bracken. And she's something called a F-O-X. She's lovely, with a reddish brown coat and bright eyes. I'm getting used to her smell. It's just a bit ... different. And her cubs are so gor-ge-ous!'

★★ 4 ★★

When he was faced with a pack of hounds:
'Oh, help! There are so many of them – all lolling tongues, big sharp teeth and waggy tails. I hope they aren't hungry! I can't stop thinking of kitten sandwiches. Do hounds even eat sandwiches? Just a minute. Waggy tails means they're friendly. They are all grinning. Phew! Thank goodness they want to make friends. They are really rather handsome, with their shiny coats, floppy ears and wet noses. Hi, doggies. Good doggies!'

Flame likes horses and ponies, but they can sometimes be nervous of him. Perhaps they sense that the tiny kitten in disguise is really a majestic young white lion. Flame is quite confident around ponies, even though they are so much bigger than him. He has been brave enough to ride one – with a human friend. Sometimes, he can tell how horses are feeling and can even read their thoughts, but only when he feels a special bond with a particular pony or horse.

Whose Hobby?

Follow these trails to match Flame's friends to their favourite hobbies. When you find the answers, fill them in below.

Olivia's hobby is: ______________________.

Abi's hobby is: ______________________.

Zoe's hobby is: ______________________.

Answers on last page

What Comes Next?

Look carefully at each pattern and see if you can guess what should come next.

Answers on last page

Codeword Conundrum

Flame has sent a coded message to Cirrus.
Use the grid below to work out what it says.

A	B	C	D	E	F	G	H	I
✡	❂	✱	❄	✚	❅	✺	❉	✖

J	K	L	M	N	O	P	Q	R
●	■	✾	▲	✲	◆	❖	◗	✙

S	T	U	V	W	X	Y	Z
▣	○	➡	◁	▼	☒	◉	⬇

Answers on last page

Looking After Your Cat

Just like Flame, any cat that you own or look after will rely on you for its welfare. Remember: a cat that is properly cared for (and loved!) is a happy cat.

Feeding

Feed your cat a nutritionally balanced cat food at least once a day (most owners feed their cats twice a day).

Provide plenty of drinking water for your cat and remember to clean the water and food bowls regularly.

General Health

Kittens should be vaccinated against disease at around eight weeks of age. Register your cat with a vet and check with them about vaccination and all other health matters.

Sleeping

While cats love to be sociable, they also like to get away from people and find a cosy spot to sleep in. A cat bed or cardboard box lined with a blanket or newspaper tucked away in a cupboard, or anywhere dark and quiet, will provide a perfect hideaway for your cat.

Grooming

Most cats will groom themselves but long-haired cats may need combing or brushing a few times a week.

All cats love to be groomed and stroked and it's a great way to bond with your feline friend!

Out and About

If you own a cat, make sure they wear a collar and identification tag with their name and your telephone number on it. Then if they do stray or get lost you can easily be contacted.

Cats can be alarmed by loud noises so keep your cat indoors during thunderstorms and firework displays.

When transporting cats, keep them in a secure carrier as they may become nervous and try to escape.

Holidays

Think about how best to look after your cat when you go away on holiday. There may be a local cattery or you could ask a trusted friend or a home-feeding service to feed your cat.

Magic Kitten

Double Trouble

Kim discovers how to cope with
her mean cousin when a fluffy silver
tabby kitten comes to stay . . .

SUE BENTLEY

Magic Kitten
Double Trouble

A sweet silver tabby kitten needs a friend!

puffin.co.uk

Magic Kitten

A Summer Spell

Lisa's boring visit to her aunt is transformed when she finds a tiny marmalade kitten in a barn . . .

puffin.co.uk

Answers

Wordsearch Wonder

O	S	A	C	I	D	S	E	I	N	O	P
E	R	C	I	L	I	S	D	U	I	S	A
G	S	N	I	E	R	E	L	D	D	A	S
Y	A	T	I	E	E	U	F	A	C	V	P
M	C	C	A	M	A	P	I	T	U	L	M
K	R	S	I	B	O	T	D	I	G	N	U
H	R	T	I	L	L	A	C	S	U	M	J
A	O	L	L	T	P	E	L	E	D	A	W
N	D	A	R	M	C	O	R	E	D	I	O
A	G	O	S	S	I	B	O	R	E	E	H
M	T	Y	R	J	O	D	P	H	U	R	S
G	U	I	S	O	N	I	M	O	L	A	P

Mixed-up Magic Words

1. cinema **2.** tickle **3.** female
4. magnet **5.** mitten **6.** climate
7. angel **8.** fake

Whose Hobby?

Olivia's hobby is ballet.
Abi's hobby is netball.
Zoe's hobby is riding.

Answers

What Comes Next?

Codeword Conundrum

The message reads:

Is it safe to return and claim the Lion Throne?

For lots more Magic Kitten fun, visit

www.puffin.co.uk/suebentley